PET PARABLES

~ VOLUME 1 ~

PET PARABLES

VOLUME 1

THE CAT WHO SMELLED LIKE CABBAGE
THE DUCK WHO QUACKED BUBBLES

BY NETA JACKSON

ILLUSTRATED BY ANNE GAVITT

KREGEL Kidzone
Where Kids are number One

Pet Parables: Volume 1

Text © 1993, 2004 by Neta Jackson
Illustrations © 1993, 2004 by Anne Gavitt

Published by Kregel Publications, P.O. Box 2607, Grand Rapids, MI 49501.

ISBN   0-8254-2938-2

Printed in China

THE
CAT WHO SMELLED
LIKE CABBAGE

"Be humble and consider others more important than yourselves."
Philippians 2:3b (CEV)

Black Cat stretched her hind legs wa-a-y back, sniffed the morning air with her button nose, then trotted toward the house next door. Her friend, Siamese Cat, was there warming herself in a sunny spot on the porch railing.

"Why, hello, Black Cat," she said, as Black Cat bounded up the porch steps. "Whatever are you so frisky for?"

"Because it's a beautiful day!" exclaimed Black Cat, hopping up onto the railing beside her friend.

"It's a *horrible* day. Can't you smell the cabbage cooking across the street?" Siamese Cat licked her fur with her dainty tongue. "But then, I suppose you don't have a nose as sensitive as mine. Mixed breeds never do."

Black Cat sighed. "No, I suppose not. There are times I wish I knew what sort of family I came from, but . . ."

8

Siamese Cat purred soothingly. "There, there, don't worry about it. You are beautiful just the same. And you belong to a nice Family, even though the Man is a Small Businessman instead of a Doctor like my Family's Man."

Black Cat started to say something, but Siamese Cat suddenly stiffened. Black Cat looked across the street and saw a large gray cat trotting up the sidewalk of the house that smelled like cabbage.

"You can be glad you aren't Alley Cat over there," sniffed Siamese Cat. "Now *there* is somebody you should stay away from."

Black Cat nodded, but said, "Why?"

"*Because* . . . that's why! She lives across the street, for one thing. For another thing, she doesn't really *live* there—I mean, she doesn't really belong to that Family. They just give her scraps now and then."

Black Cat thought of the Golden Nugget Cat Food she ate by the bowlful every morning.

"Besides," Siamese Cat went on, licking her milky-brown fur again, "she is so ugly. There's not a graceful bone in her body—lack of good breeding, of course."

Black Cat began licking her own soft fur, grateful that she was not ugly like Alley Cat.

"But the worst thing of all," Siamese Cat suddenly hissed, "is . . ."

"Is what?" Black Cat stopped her tongue in mid-lick and looked at her friend with wide eyes.

"The way she roams around the neighborhood at night while decent cats like us are in bed where they should be. Disgraceful."

Siamese Cat finished her bath. "Well, enough of that. I forgot to ask how your children are."

"Children!" Black Cat exclaimed. "Oh, I'm glad you reminded me. They are getting so playful. If I don't hurry back home, they will be getting into everything." She jumped off the porch railing and hurried down the steps. "Shall we go for our walk as usual this afternoon?" she called back.

"Of course, dearie," Siamese Cat purred. As Black Cat trotted away, Siamese Cat sighed. "Children. What a bother. I'm glad they're not mine."

Black Cat's kittens fussed over their lunch, then they socked and played with each other, and would not settle down. Finally, the last one dropped off to sleep.

Black Cat sighed. *They really are good children*, she thought fondly, *but how do I get them to settle down for their naps after lunch?* She took one last look, and padded softly out of the house so she wouldn't be late for her walk with Siamese Cat.

I would like to ask Siamese Cat for advice, she thought as she headed down the sidewalk, *but I know just what she'd say.* "That's your *problem, dearie!*"

Just then Black Cat thought she heard a tiny meow. Then everything happened so fast—the blast of a car horn, a large gray blur streaking past her. Just as quickly, it was all over, and Alley Cat was gently dropping one of Black Cat's children at her feet.

"What happened?" Black Cat gasped. She anxiously licked her kitten all over. It didn't seem to be hurt at all.

"I'm not sure," Alley Cat said shyly. "I think your kitten followed you out of the house. When I saw it toddling into the street . . . well, I didn't wait to find out if you knew it was behind you or not."

"Oh. Well, thank you very much." Black Cat was beginning to feel uncomfortable. Up close, Alley Cat really was ugly. Her left ear was ragged, and she wasn't gray at all, but black and yellow and brown and white. And Black Cat had to admit that Alley Cat definitely smelled like cabbage.

"Black Cat!" It was Siamese Cat calling from her porch-railing throne. "You are late for our walk!"

"Oh, I must be going," Black Cat said. "But I do want to thank you for rescuing my kitten. Really I do."

"I'm glad it's not hurt," Alley Cat said softly. "You see, I have kittens, too."

Black Cat stopped in her tracks and blinked in surprise. "You do?"

"Oh, yes." Alley Cat smiled shyly. "Eight of them, and they're almost four weeks old."

"But . . ." Black Cat's curiosity got the best of her. "But . . . where do you live? I mean, where do you keep your kittens?"

"In the bushes behind the house across the street." Alley Cat saw the horrified look on Black Cat's face and tried to explain. "Yes, it gets cold at night. But the Landlord won't let the Family who lives there have any pets. At least they don't chase me out of their yard like all the other Families on this block do."

"Black Cat!" Siamese Cat called again. Black Cat looked anxiously in her direction, but again her curiosity got the better of her.

"But wouldn't it be better to find a . . . well, a better Family to live with?"

"A better Family?" Alley Cat gave a short laugh. "Sure, it would be nice to have a Family that dished out food three times a day! But who's going to adopt a cat as ugly as I am?"

Black Cat didn't know what to say.

"But," Alley Cat went on, "I'm not sure if there is a 'better' Family. They've got seven kids and barely enough food to go around the table, but they always give some little scraps to me, and a kind word and a pat. Of course, those scraps don't feed eight kittens, so . . ."

". . . so you go around the neighborhood at night, trying to find food," Black Cat finished, a new look coming into her face.

"Why, yes," Alley Cat said, surprised. "How did you know?"

"Black Cat! Remember what I told you," Siamese Cat scolded crossly from her house.

Alley Cat sighed. "I guess I know how you know. I suppose you think what I do is awful."

Black Cat just stood there, thinking very hard.

Alley Cat looked embarrassed. "Well, I guess I'll go back across the street. You have a very beautiful kitten."

"Wait!" Black Cat said. "Have you had very many kittens?"

Alley Cat laughed. "This is my fifth litter—and that makes thirty-two children all together!"

Black Cat grinned shyly. "This is just my first—six children in all—and I'm having a terrible time with the nap problem. Have you found any solutions with yours?"

"Oh my, yes. I . . ." Alley Cat stopped. "Are you sure you want to stay and talk? I mean, your friend . . ."

"Yes, I'm sure. But first, there's a place under my Family's porch where an air vent from the furnace opens out. If you moved your kittens under there, they would surely be warm enough at night. C'mon, I'll show you."

"Black Cat!" screeched Siamese Cat.

24

"I'll be back in a few minutes," Black Cat called back. "I have something important to do first." She picked up her kitten and led the way back up the sidewalk.

"Do you like cabbage?" Alley Cat asked, as the two cats trotted toward Black Cat's house. Black Cat could only grunt because she carried her kitten with her mouth. "Well, it tastes much better than it smells," Alley Cat continued. "I really have grown to like it—you'll have to come over and try it sometime. And wait'll you see my kittens . . ."

Black Cat smiled to herself, as her new friend talked on and on.

TO PARENTS AND TEACHERS:

Prejudice is a big word for young children to comprehend—but prejudice begins at an early age. Young children often have a warm acceptance of all sorts of people, but this acceptance is easily influenced by the attitudes and reactions of others. Also, if children feel insecure about their own identity or struggle with low self-esteem, they may try to build up their own importance by putting other people down.

After reading the story of Black Cat, Siamese Cat, and Alley Cat aloud to your child, you may want to use the following questions to discuss how we think about or relate to people who may look different or do things differently.

- Why didn't Siamese Cat want Black Cat to be friends with Alley Cat?
- How did Black Cat feel about Alley Cat when she actually talked to her?
- What happens when we listen to gossip about someone who seems a little different from us?
- How does God want us to treat people who are different from us?
- Do you know someone who needs a friend? Could you be that friend?

THE DUCK WHO QUACKED BUBBLES

"*Do everything without complaining or arguing,
so that you may become blameless and pure. . . .*"
Philippians 2:14–15a

The space under the front porch of the farmhouse was cool and shady. The straw in the old blueberry box was clean and sweet-smelling. So why did Grumble feel all hot and squashed?

The little duckling opened her eyes. All she could see were fuzzy yellow feathers in her face.

"Cuddle!" she quacked loudly. "I can't take a nap if you're lying on top of me!"

Grumble's sister wiggled over in the nest. This woke up all the other ducklings in the blueberry box.

"Mama," yawned Noodle. "Grumble's complaining again and waking us up."

"Shhh," hissed Mama Duck. She wasn't ready to get up yet.

But by now all six ducklings were awake and falling out of the nest—Noodle, Puddle, Waddle, Cuddle, Dawdle, and Grumble. Mama Duck sighed and waddled out from under the porch into the bright sunshine.

The six ducklings scurried close behind her. They all looked exactly alike, but each one was special. Noodle liked to eat, Puddle would rather swim, and—

"I saw that bug first!" Grumble quacked just then. "Mama, Noodle ate the bug that I was going to eat!"

. . . And then there was Grumble. Mama Duck pretended not to hear Grumble's complaints and marched toward the cheerful sign that said, "Patty's Blueberry Patch." Beside the fruit stand were rows and rows of thick blueberry bushes. Nearby was a pond. The water sparkled in the sunlight.

"Let's go swimming, Mama!" said Puddle.

"Yes! Yes!" quacked the other ducklings.

"Yeah, sure," muttered Grumble. "Puddle wants to go swimming so he can splash me again, just like he did yesterday."

"Let's visit the fruit stand first," said Mama Duck. "Patty might have some berries we can eat for a snack."

Just then, Waddle bumped into Grumble and knocked her over.

"Waddle!" quacked Grumble loudly. "Watch where you're going! Can't you walk in a straight line?"

"Sorry, Grumble," Waddle mumbled and waddled off again.

Patty was busy waiting on customers who had stopped at the blueberry patch. Mama Duck and the ducklings looked for stray blueberries that might have dropped on the ground.

Grumble had just found a plump, juicy blueberry when she heard a child squeal. "Look! Duckies!" Before Grumble knew what was happening, childish hands smeared with blueberries had grabbed her up.

Grumble kicked and squawked. "Put me down! Put me down!" she quacked. "You're getting blueberries all over my nice yellow feathers!"

The child giggled. Grumble's complaints just sounded like, "Quack! Quack! Quack!" Finally, the child put the duckling down and ran to get in the car.

"Just look at my poor feathers," Grumble complained. The other ducklings tried not to laugh. But Grumble did look funny with purple feathers.

"Come on, come on!" scolded Grumble. "I want to go swimming now. I need to take a bath." She marched as fast as she could toward the pond. "Stupid children," she grumbled.

"Wait, Grumble," she heard Mama Duck call. Dawdle was coming slowly, bringing up the rear.

"Why do we always have to wait for Dawdle?" Grumble complained. "Wait, wait, wait. I don't want to wait." The duckling paced back and forth, grumbling to herself.

"Noodle eats my bugs. Cuddle leans on me in the nest. Waddle is always bumping into me. Puddle splashes me whenever we go swimming. Dawdle is always making us late."

Grumble was so busy grumbling that she didn't notice that Mama Duck and the other ducklings had caught up to her and were listening to her complaints.

"Are you finished complaining?" asked Mama Duck patiently. "If so, let's go swimming now." And the big white duck waddled over to the pond and settled gracefully into the water.

Grumble was about to follow when Noodle and the other ducklings stopped her. "Just go away, Grumble," said Noodle. "You're no fun. You're always complaining."

"Yeah," said Puddle. "We don't want to play with you."

"Yeah," said Waddle and Cuddle.

"Yeah," said Dawdle. "Go away."

Then the other five ducklings ran into the pond after Mama Duck.

Grumble stared after her brothers and sisters. *Well!* she thought. *They can't tell me what to do.* So she walked over to the pond and hopped into the water. She wiggled and splashed until she had washed all the blueberry juice off her feathers.

Then she looked around. The others were playing hide and seek among the lily pads. It looked like fun. But if they didn't want to play with her, she could have fun all by herself.

Grumble got out of the pond, shook all the water out of her feathers, and wandered back toward the fruit stand. A woman and several children were waiting in the car while a man was buying a big box of blueberries.

Then Grumble saw something she hadn't seen before. A big box-thing made of wooden slats was also standing in the driveway. It had a wooden door in back that rested on the ground, making a little ramp.

Just then Grumble got an idea. The other ducklings had said, "Go away." Well! She would show them. She would hide in the box and make them think she had gone away; *then* they'd be sorry.

Grumble ran as fast as she could up the little ramp. The wooden box was full of sleeping bags and suitcases and sand pails and fishing rods. She squeezed between a sleeping bag and a sand pail and peeked out between the wooden slats.

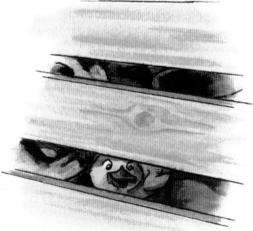

The man was coming toward the box with the flat of blueberries. He set it inside the box-thing, slammed the wooden door shut, and got back in the car. The car pulled out of the driveway onto the road.

All of a sudden Grumble was scared. The wooden box was moving too! The car was pulling it. She had hidden in a trailer by mistake, and the trailer was going away! The car drove past the pond where Mama Duck and the ducklings were still swimming and splashing. Grumble quacked and quacked. "Mama! Mama! Help me!" But Mama Duck and the ducklings couldn't hear her.

Grumble didn't want to go away. She wanted her Mama. She wanted Noodle and Puddle and Waddle and Cuddle and Dawdle. She wanted out of there!

But the car and trailer drove down the road until Grumble couldn't see the pond or Patty's Blueberry Patch any more.

41

Grumble didn't know what to do. "Quack," she sniffed, as the trees and fields rushed past. If only she could be home again, she would try very hard not to complain so much. She wanted to play with her brothers and sisters—even if she did get bumped or splashed or squashed in the nest.

Then she felt the car slowing down. She looked out between the wooden slats. The car was pulling into a gas station. "Quack! Quack! Quack!" she said loudly. "Quack! Quack! Quack!"

"I hear quacking in our trailer," said a woman's voice. "Whatever can it be?"

The trailer door was opened. "Why, it's a duckling," said a man's voice.

"Can we keep it?" said children's voices. "Please?"

"I think it got into our trailer back at the blueberry stand," said the man. "We'll have to take it back."

"Awww," said the children.

Small hands reached for the duckling. But this time Grumble didn't struggle. She sat quietly on a child's lap as the car drove back the way it had just come.

Soon the car and trailer pulled into Patty's Blueberry Patch again. Childish hands set Grumble gently on the ground.

Mama Duck and all the other ducklings came running. "Grumble! Where have you been! We've been looking all over for you. We were worried!"

"We didn't really mean for you to go away," said Noodle.

Grumble was so happy to be home that she couldn't even quack.

"Come on!" said Puddle. "Let's go back to the pond and play hide and seek. You can be 'it.'"

The ducklings scurried back into the water. Grumble paddled happily toward the lily pads. But just then Waddle bumped into her.

"Waddle!" Grumble protested.

Then she stopped. If she complained, maybe Waddle wouldn't want to play with her. So instead of grumbling, she dipped her head under the water and stuck her tail up in the air. Only bubbles came up.

The ducklings had fun playing hide and seek. When Mama Duck quacked for them to come in, Grumble paddled lazily, letting the sun dry off her head and back. Just then Puddle beat his wings and shook water out of his feathers—and got Grumble all wet again!

"Pud—!" Grumble started to say crossly. But instead she stood on her head in the water, and only bubbles came up.

The other ducklings laughed. "Look, Mama!" they called to Mama Duck. "Grumble is quacking bubbles!"

Mama Duck had been watching as Grumble tried not to complain. "Maybe Grumble isn't a very good name for a certain duckling I know. Maybe we should call her Bubbles instead!"

Noodle and Puddle and Waddle and Cuddle and Dawdle cheered. "Yes, let's call her Bubbles instead."

Grumble was so happy that she stood on her head and quacked under water.

Bubble, bubble, bubble.

 # TO THE PARENT AND TEACHERS:

Some children are generally good-natured and not bothered by much. Then there are children who can always find fault with something. Children's literature celebrates both of these extremes with characters like Pollyanna (the "sunshine girl") and Grumpy in the story of Snow White.

Most children fall somewhere in between. Everyone has a bad day now and then when nothing seems to go right. At these times, some tolerance and patience can help a grumpy child over the hump.

But complaining can also become a bad habit. Children need to realize that other people don't enjoy being around someone who is always grumbling.

After reading the story of Grumble aloud to your child, you may want to use the following questions to talk about how it feels when someone gripes a lot, and how to break the habit of complaining:

- Why didn't the other ducklings want to play with Grumble?
- How did the other ducklings feel when Grumble tried to stop complaining?
- How do our friends feel when we complain about everything?
- What do you think God wants us to do when we feel like complaining?
- The next time you feel like complaining, what could you do instead?